WORRY
JUICE

YUM

ABC

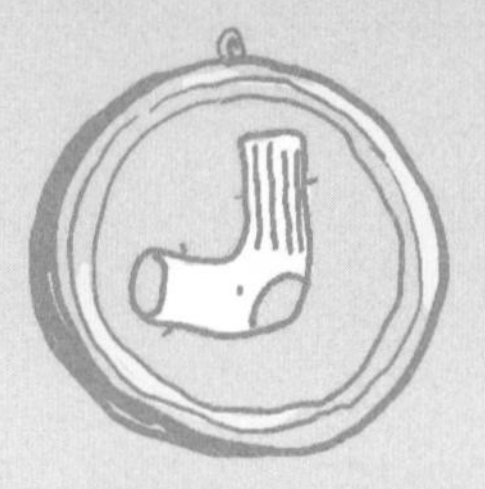

STRAW
BERRY

MOM

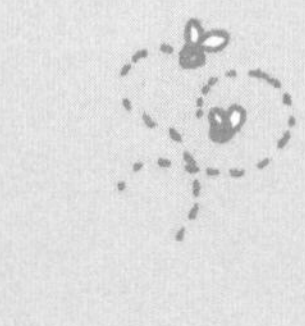

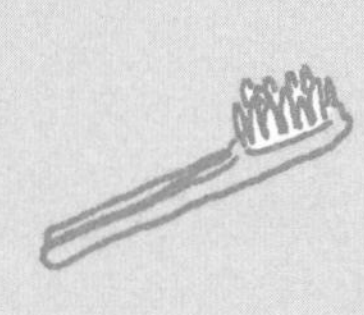

Zilot
/'zi-lit/
& Other
Important
Rhymes

RAH
START THE SHOW!

by
BOB
ODENKIRK

with illustrations by
ERIN
ODENKIRK

with extra, added cherry-on-top contributions by
NATE ODENKIRK and NAOMI ODENKIRK

Little, Brown and Company
New York Boston

ABOUT THIS BOOK

The illustrations for this book were done in pen and digital color. This book was edited by Mary-Kate Gaudet and Farrin Jacobs, art directed by Sasha Illingworth, and designed by Neil Swaab. The production was supervised by Virginia Lawther, and the production editor was Andy Ball. The text was set in Clifford Nine, and the display type is P22 Garamouche.

Little, Brown and Company
Hachette Book Group
1290 Avenue of the Americas, New York, NY 10104
Visit us at LBYR.com

First Edition: October 2023

Little, Brown and Company is a division of Hachette Book Group, Inc.
The Little, Brown name and logo are trademarks of Hachette Book Group, Inc.

The publisher is not responsible for websites (or their content) that are not owned by the publisher.

Library of Congress Cataloging-in-Publication Data

Names: Odenkirk, Bob, 1962– author. | Odenkirk, Erin, illustrator. | Odenkirk, Nate, contributor. | Odenkirk, Naomi, contributor. • Title: Zilot & other important rhymes / by Bob Odenkirk with illustrations by Erin Odenkirk and contributions by Nate Odenkirk and Naomi Odenkirk. Other titles: Zilot and other important rhymes • Description: First edition. | New York : Little, Brown and Company, 2023. | Audience: Ages 6 and Up. | Summary: "A collection of humorous and heartfelt poetry for children and adults" —Provided by publisher. • Identifiers: LCCN 2022055515 (print) | LCCN 2022055516 (ebook) | ISBN 9780316438506 (hardcover) | ISBN 9780316567251 (ebook) | ISBN 9780316567268 (kindle edition) | ISBN 9780316567275 (nook edition) • Subjects: LCSH: Children's poetry, American. | Humorous poetry, American. | CYAC: American poetry. | Humorous poetry. | LCGFT: Humorous poetry. • Classification: LCC PS3615.D4654 Z35 2023 (print) | LCC PS3615.D4654 (ebook) | DDC 811/.6—dc23/eng/20230130 • LC record available at https://lccn.loc.gov/2022055515
LC ebook record available at https://lccn.loc.gov/2022055516

ISBNs: 978-0-316-43850-6 (hardcover), 978-0-316-56725-1 (ebook)

PRINTED IN CHINA

APS

10 9 8 7 6 5 4 3 2 1

For Naomi, who inspires and encourages us,

and to all people who read to kids!

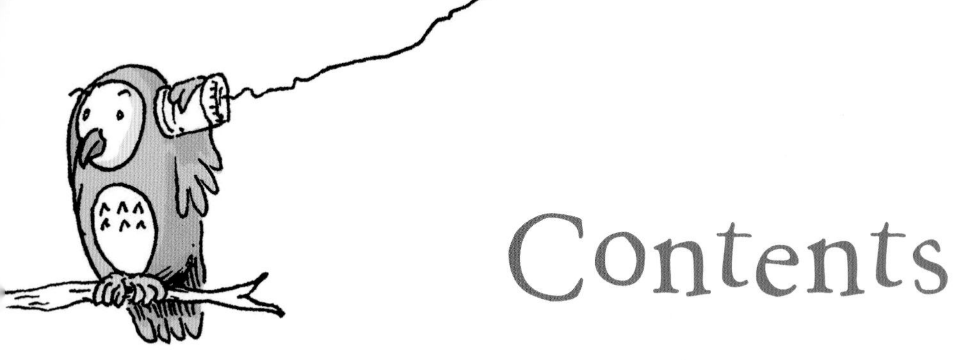

Contents

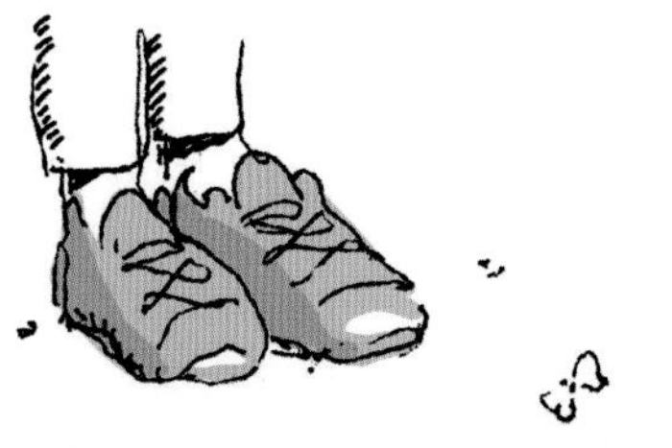

BUMBER-
SHOOOP
SEED-
LING!

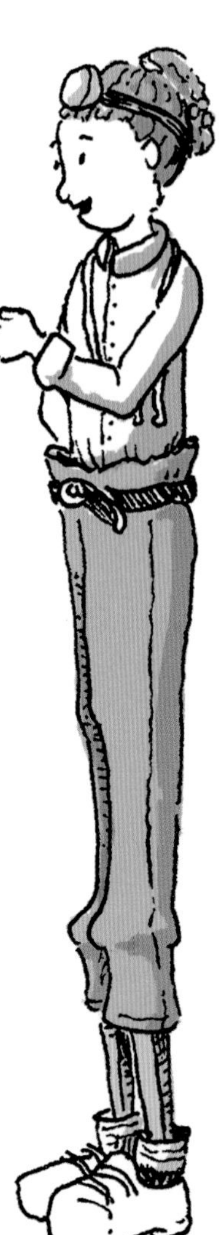

Zilot
/'zi-lit/
& Other
Important
Rhymes

Zilot

A zilot is an indoor fort,
a home inside your home.
You can build one on a rainy day
so you can be alone.
But make it bigger if you want to,
and have a friend or pet in.
Parents can drop by as well—
they'll have to crouch to get in.

Chairs or couch provide the sides,
a blanket makes the roof,
then crawl inside—and *Hooray!*
Here's your chance to be aloof!

Bring a flashlight so you can read a book,
this one will do—keep readin'.
Or make a shadow rabbit with your hand
(real rabbits need constant feedin').

In a zilot you can calm way down
and feel what you're feeling.
You can close your eyes
and look inside
and watch your thoughts unreeling.

But CAREFUL!

Don't get rambunctious,
don't clutter or overfill it.
Be cool and mellow,
and you won't compromise
the integrity of the zilot!

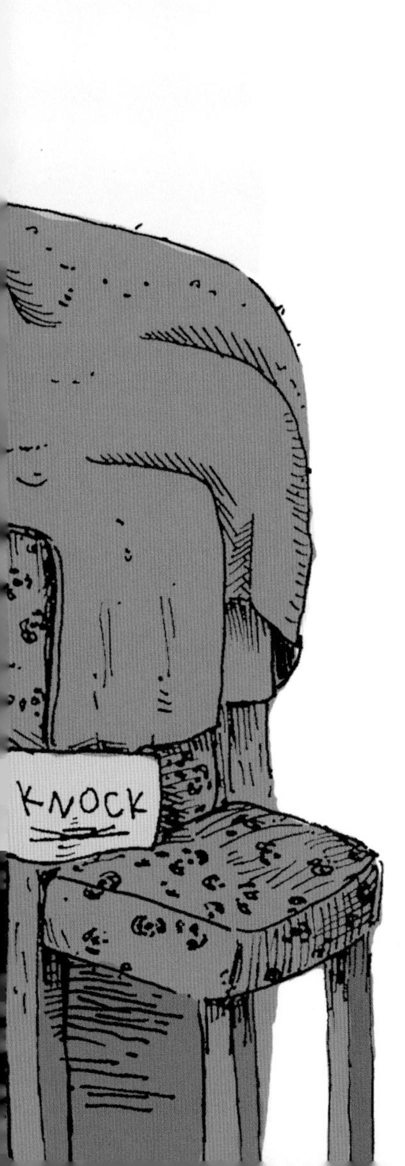

Oh Shoelace, My Shoelace!

It was a dirty old thing,
but I never wanted one newer.
Did I mention I found it
in the street, by the sewer?

It was long and thin.
"Threadbare," you might say.
Its threads were all shredded
and on full display.

The hours I spent with it!
Tying knots by the score.
And the untying part
used up even more.

I waved it around.
The cat tried to swat it,
the lace and I laughed.
That ol' cat never got it!

I slept with it and sang to it.
I kept it so close.
My mother shook her head.
"That old lace, it's just gross."

Perhaps I took it too far
when I insisted she kiss it.
Now she's thrown it away.
All my life I will miss it.

Willy Whimble

It's true, I am
a diminutive man.
My home suits me well.
It's an old tuna can.

I just mopped the floor;
be careful, don't slip.
I've shined it up nicely
with an old Q-tip.
I've taken a bath.
My bathtub's a thimble.
Oh, hello! My name is Willy,
short for "William T. Whimble."

My hat is minute,
it's mini, it's wee.
But my head's full of thoughts
rolling on infinitely.
Even better, my heart
is big as can be.

Come inside,
stay for dinner.
I'll roast us a pea!

A Day at the Park

Today, children, we'll visit the park.
We'll be there all day
and home before dark.

Now, there are some rules
because we'll be outside.
It's okay to play seek
but never to hide.

Don't climb the trees.
Don't befriend the bees.
Don't sway in the breeze.
Let's not skin any knees.

No frolicking, no hollering.
No leading, no following.
No hopping, no scotching.
And definitely no bird-watching!

Stay on the bus,
no talking, no play.
We'll park in the parking lot.
Oh, what a fun day!

Wishful

I saved up my coins,
put 'em in jars,
to get a new bike
to replace my stinky old car.

I saved and I saved
penny after penny
'til a new bike was gettable—
I'd saved up so many!

So I went to a well
and dumped all the coins in
and wished for a ten-speed
with shiny wheels that would spin.

My plan was goof-proof,
I ain't no dunce.
There was no way my wish
wouldn't be granted at once!

It's been a year, still no bike,
so, I g u e s s . . .
I'll save up lots more, then—
cross my fingers, pick a clover (four-leafed), find an eyelash, kiss a turtle on the lips, save a ladybug's life, throw my coins in a *new* fountain and *wish for the best*!

Lollygagging

There's not enough lollygagging
going on around here,
and daydreams are in short supply.
The whole week is jammed
with to-dos and to-don'ts.
No one's gazing at clouds in the sky.

THERE'S SO MUCH NONSENSE TO ACCOMPLISH!
I simply can't do it all alone . . .

I'll think stray thoughts and you mutter drivel.
You walk in circles and I'll tunelessly whistle.
We'll bandy about the most pointless of piffle
and cram this day full
of jabber and jibble.

We'll aim to aim aimlessly
and traipse about spaciously
and fart around graciously
and fritter tenaciously.

Let's not focus nor work
on what's "necessary" or "needed."
Let's get down to beeswax
and get our *lollygagging* completed!

One Nice Thing a Day

I poured syrup on Jeff's couch
to make it a little sweeter.
I vacuumed up Suzie's puzzle pieces
to make her room a little neater.

I stapled the pages of Aidan's books together,
no more paper cuts for my pal's fingers.
I traced my hand onto Cornelia's front door,
so the fond memory of our playdate lingers.

Follow my example and you'll be known
as a thoughtful pal not a grouch.
Do one nice thing every day—
and whatever you do,
don't sit on Jeff's couch!

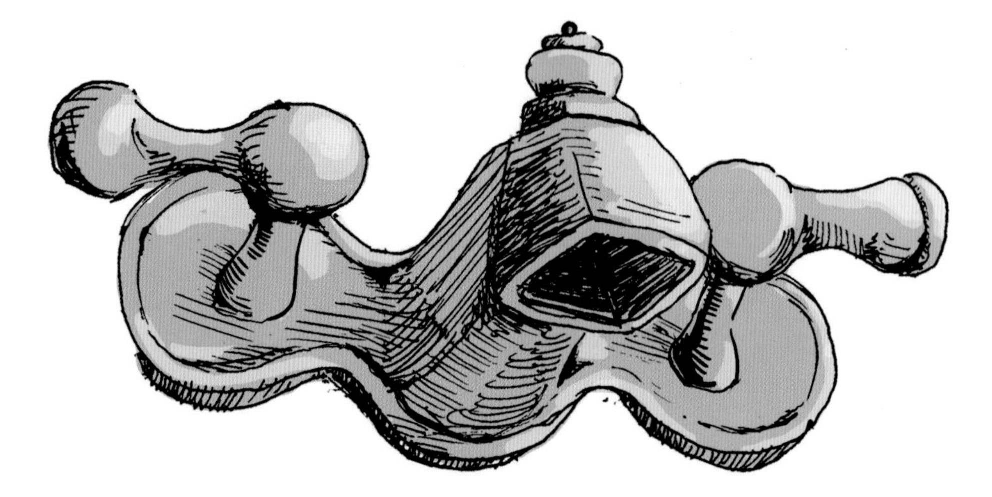

Goodbye, Dirt

Turn the faucet on.
It's time to say, "G'bye!,"
"Au revoir!," "Bon voyage!,"
old pals of mine.

To the grease in my hair,
the jam 'twixt my toes,
the gunk on my hands,
dried schnots round my nose,

the crusts in my eyes,
the flakes in my ears,
a heartfelt goodbye,
I'll miss you, my dears.

Tomorrow I'll roll around in muck,
stomp about in scum,
splash in every puddle—
and make all new chums!

THE LORAX
POE FOR DUMMIES
CALVIN & HOBBES
MUTTS
The Tale of DESPEREAUX

Gooby

I know a little dog by the name of Gooby.
Most nights before bed
she gets the zips and zoomies.

Gooby whips round the room
with great vigor and zeal.
The parents don't like it,
but I know how she feels.

The Little Table

"Sit at the little table with the little kids, Lavelle."
But I'm a big kid now. I'm eleven—nearly twelve!
Oh, well . . .

I slump and slouch
and force my knees akimbo
to fit under the table
as low as I can limbo.

Around the little table where I have been banished
my tablemates look hungry,
forlorn and famished.
Their food falls off their spoons.
They are thin, getting thinner
because no adults have bothered
to cut up their dinner.

“Help?” a suffering tyke sputters.
I’m the only one with a knife,
the kind for spreading butter.
I cut up her carrots and meat
and vanquish her woes.
She needs no assistance
hoisting her mashed potatoes.
I fix everyones’ plates to make their food scoopable,
eatable, right-sized, and easily chewable.

When dinner’s done, I’m stuffed with pride and turkey
as full as I am able.
The only creature fuller
sits below me,
at a littler table.

Unsteady Job

I go to work,
my head held high,
notepad in hand.
I watch the sky.
I keep track of clouds
and the shapes they're making.
I write down whatever
the wind's creating.
I love the fact that
they're constantly changing!

But sometimes I'm stumped
by those nimbus clumps
on a blustery day
  when I want to say:

"Settle down!
Pick a shape!
Or just blow away!"

Read the Label

I brushed
my teeth just now
with the toothpaste
called Ka-pow!

It's supposed to remove stains
and sugary rot,
anything you ate
but now have forgot—
and to utterly clean
any speckles of beef—
but it worked too well.
It took off my teef.

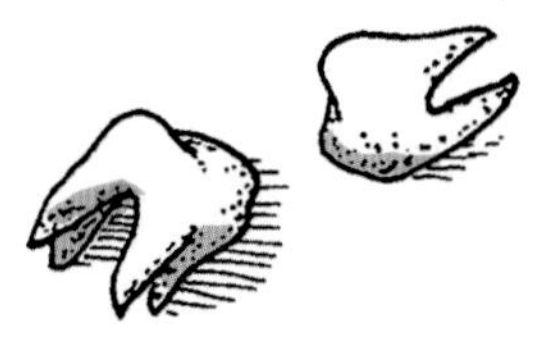

WARNING:
PROLONGED TOOTH BRUSH
MAY (WILL) RESULT IN COMPLETE
TOOTH LOSS. DOCTORS
SUGGEST MAXIMUM ONE (1)
BRUSH PER TOOTH. KA-POW!©
NOT RESPONSIBLE
TOOTH DAMAGE OR
A RESULT OF
KA-POW
TOOTH PASTE
CHERRY-BERRY CHOCO-MINT

To the Zoo

To the zoo in winter we go
 to see animals in the freezing cold.

The monkeys are wrapped in blankets, wearing mittens.
You can't tell if you're looking at a macaque or a gibbon!

The giraffe's curled up.
She's barely a speck.
The scarf that they gave her
couldn't scarf her whole neck.

The birds? Where's the birds?
Huddled INSIDE the trees.
(No one's flying through this freeze.)
At this point, I'll be honest,
I'd be pleased to see bees.

The elephant's in the reptile room,
you might say, "He's out of his element."
I'd love to meet him, but the door's stuck
'cause the room's crammed with elephant.

Look at this!
The penguins and polar bears
have come out to play.
They think today's the best
and most perfect-est day!

Incrementalism: A Theory

Nothing is done all at once—
nothing great, anyway.
Even climbing Mount Everest
starts with one step on one day.

And this is . . . INCREMENTALISM.
It's only a theory
until you put it in action,
so lace up your shoes
and let's get some traction.

I'm not saying that you have to climb *anything*!
Everyone has their own dream
as distinct as their laughter,
and it's not up to me to decide what you're after.

So, find a big dream,
something special and true.
Then step lots of steps
toward the thing that excites you.

But back to Mount Everest . . .

I DO wish you'd climb it.
You see, I'm headed there, too.
And I want a friend to meet me—
could it be you?

So let's agree that tomorrow,
as you walk toward school,
tell everyone you're "climbing Everest"—
I think it'd be cool.

The world is round,

so whether you head east or west,

you'll be inching—

inc r e m e n t a l l y —

toward ol' Everest.

BABY
#1

Enough about the Baby

The baby did this.
The baby did that.
The baby did something else—SO?
I was "the baby" first, ya know!

I Never Sleep

I haven't slept
for at least two years—
I ride on a blanket
steered with elephant ears.
Through the starry sky,
all night long, I fly and I fly.

That ol' sleepster, Mr. Sandman,
claims he's got my number.
He insists there'll come a day
when he'll get me to slumber!

But, for now, no time to waste—
my nights simply overflow
chasing scoundrels and being chased,
beside my monster pal Bonfiglio.

Flying, dipping, getting splashed
as we sail through saltwater skies.
No wonder when the sun comes up
I have crusts in my eyes!

I've just one regret,
grand as my nights may seem.
It's a terrible shame
that I shan't ever dream.

How Planes Work

The plane ride is an irony
with a strange and wondrous duplicity.
I shall state this conundrum with simplicity:
"IF YOU STAY IN YOUR SEAT, YOU'LL GO FAR."

If you sit and sit and sit and sit
and stay sat so long that
your bum is tired
and you feel strangely wired,
then you will find yourself unstuck,
far-flung and unmired!

The plane will land WAAAAAY over THERE,
and all you did was sit in a chair!
Don't think about it too much.
This is no time for hairsplitting.
Just get yourself a ticket
and start sit, sit, sit, sitting!

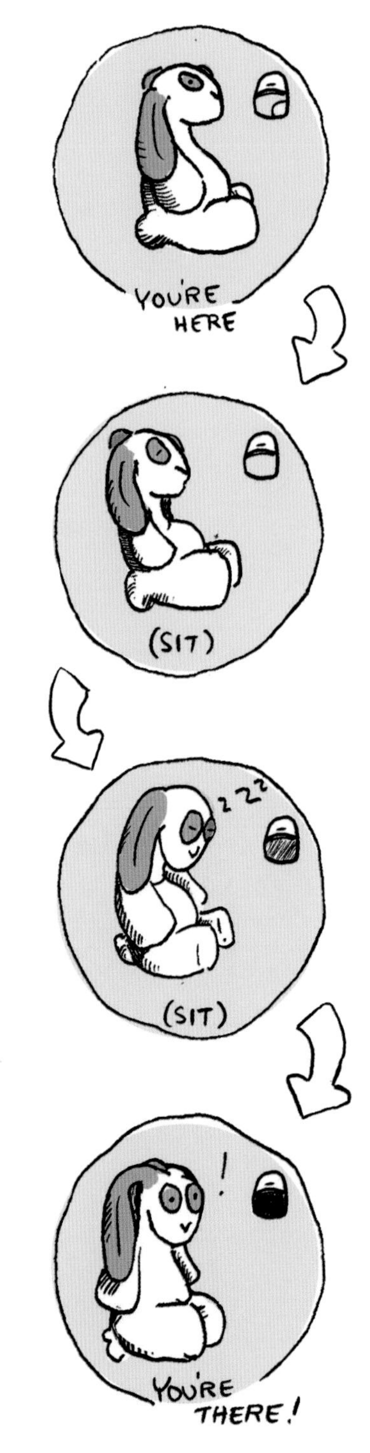

When I Grow Up

When I grow up,
I'll be a garbage truck!
Big, green, and smelly.
I'll eat trash with a metal arm,
loading garbage into my belly.

When I grow up,
I'll be a house,
with floors (at least three).
I'll be a place where people love to be,
and that way, you see, I'll never be lonely.

When I grow up,
I'll be a raindrop,
racing down from the clouds,
landing with a PLOP.
Given the chance,
I'll be the water that waters the plants.
I'll live forever; I'll never die.
I'll grow something new
with every goodbye.

Mr. Rue D. Behaviour

He is rude,
but he's our guest.
He claims he's proud
to be a pest.

We offer him cake.
He's already burping!

He asks for milk
and so begins slurping.

He pops a balloon
to keep the baby awake.

He grabs the cat by the tail
for *badness'* sake!

Oh, we want him to leave.

What will it take?

How about a whispering contest?

Whoever's quietest sticks around.

Rudy bellows and shrieks,

of course he does, he can only make BIG sounds.

And so he must go—his bindle in tow,

a glum and ridiculous clown.

Is he welcome back, the rude old dear?

Of course, he is—when we're not here!

A Frida Kahlo

Frida Kahlo knew something
that no one else knew,
and now I am going to tell that something to you.

From when she was young,
she said, "There's one thing I know.
I am who I am.
I'm a great Frida Kahlo!"

She painted and drew
and made all kinds of art
to show the feelings conjured up
in the lens of her heart.

Her eyes saw the world
slightly askew,
unique and distinct
and refreshingly true.

Now everyone loves her work,
though they put their own spin on it.
But there was a time when little Frida
was the only one in on it.

Well, you have a little Frida Kahlo yourself.

"A masterpiece!"
"Distinctive!" and
"Undeniably new!"

Your Frida Kahlo
is someone called
You!

Tweeting Birds

Outside my window,
the birdies are tweeting.
Science tells us
it's their manner of speaking,
of commenting and sharing
the news of the day.
What's the weather?
Where're the worms?
In which puddle must we play?

Now, birdies, remember,
you may grouse about weather,
but only say *nice* things
about other birds' feathers.

Mud

If Mom were Finnish,
she would know
lots and lots of words for “snow.”
But we live in Mobile
where it rains ’til it floods,
so my mom has multiple words for mud!

FOUND

I FOUND A WAD OF GUM

- STICKY AND WET
- VIOLET BLUE
- HEAVILY CHEWED

I BET IT MEANS A LOT TO YOU...

SO, IF YOU'RE LOOKING FOR YOUR LOST GUM,
I'VE GOT IT SAFELY HIDDEN
(UNDER MY TONGUE)

Magic Time

The dishes in the sink
drawing flies, big and fat.
Stinky lumps in the litter box
dropped off by the cat.
Musty clothes from the hamper
crawling this way 'cross the floor.
Piles of trash barely balanced
stand guard at the door.

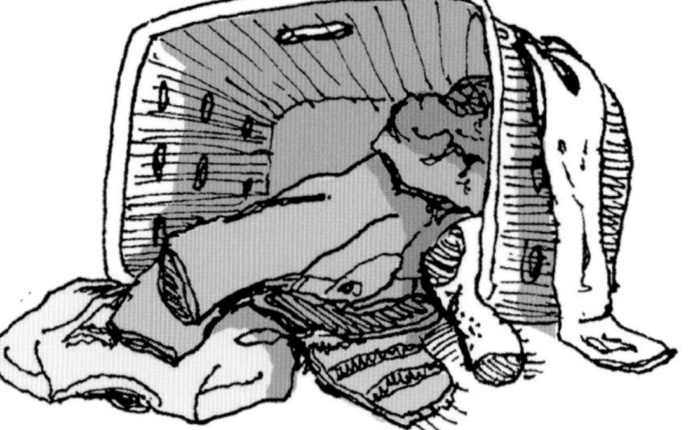

The orange juice I spilled
is starting to glisten.
It's clear to me that
this must be our mission:
I'll clean the bedroom,
you clean the kitchen—
YIKES! There's a sock
standing of its own volition
waving to me with a crusty old mitten!
It's hopeless, we're doomed.
In our catastrophic condition,
to make this mess disappear,
let's just hire a magician!

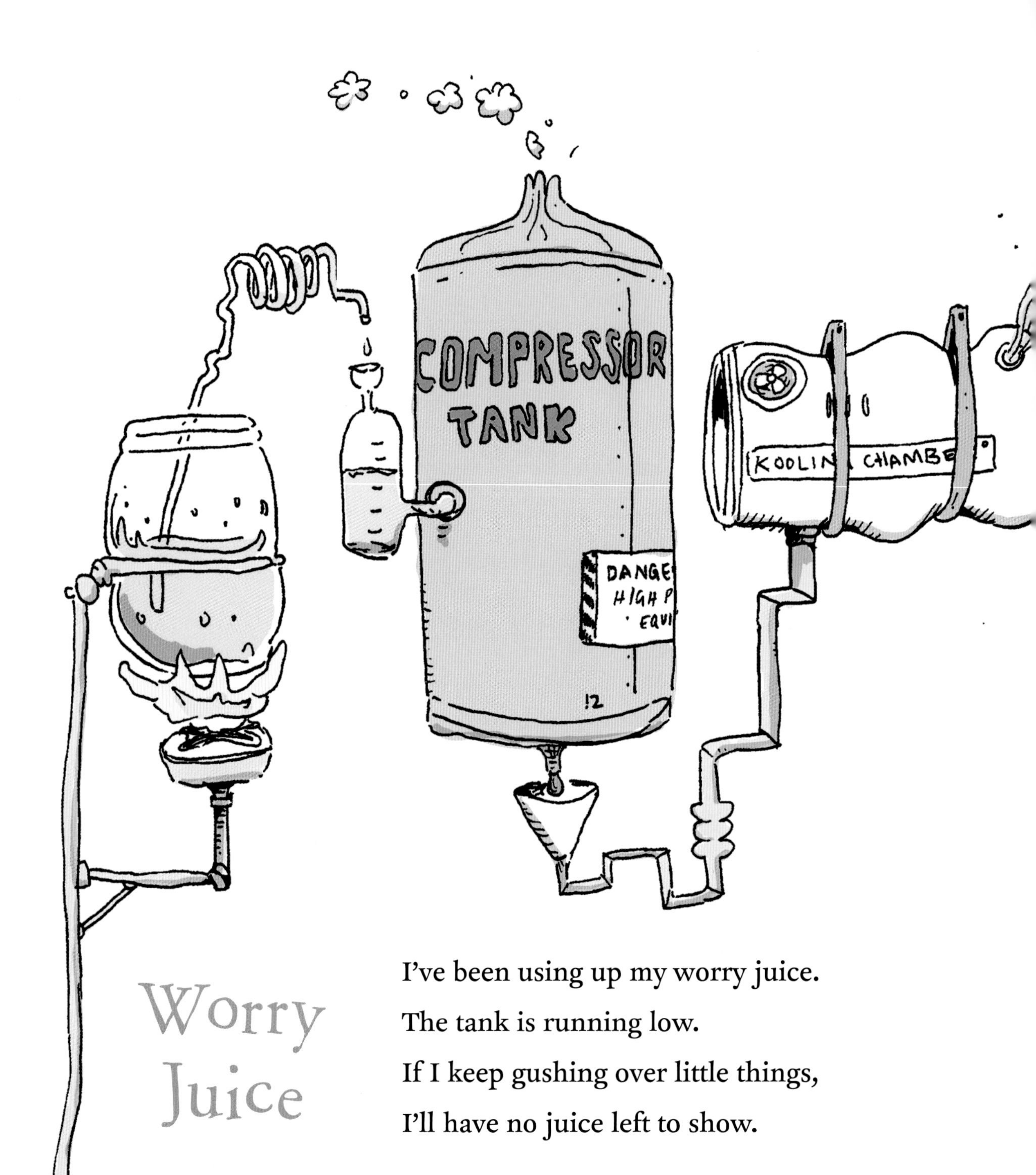

Worry Juice

I've been using up my worry juice.
The tank is running low.
If I keep gushing over little things,
I'll have no juice left to show.

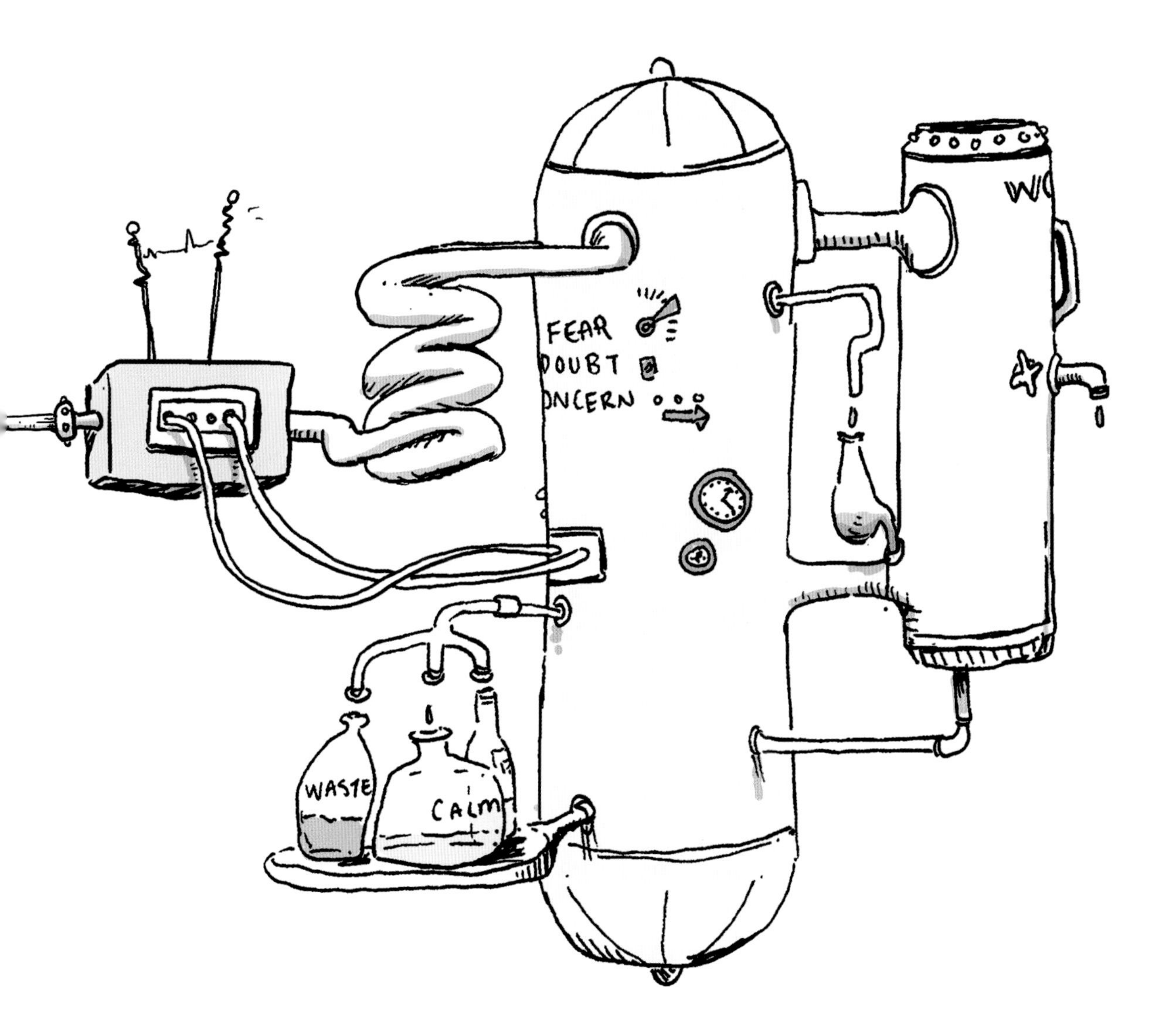

So I'm going to pat my little worries on the head
and give them a nap.
Then when there's something big to worry about,
I'll have juice left on tap.

The Perfect Scribble

My pencil did it—I barely helped.
I guess . . . I held the pencil—
there was no helpful elf.

But something happened,
something bigger than me.
And out came this scribble,
this perfect scribble you now see.

The be-all and end-all of perfection in scribbling,
no matter and no mind to any critical quibbling.

Give the pencil the credit!
I simply followed my heart.
No one else needs to like it.
I LIKE IT A LOT.

Grandma's Skin

Grandma's skin is thin and dry.
She tells me about it and I don't know why.
I also know that her temperature's low.
I'm not sure what I should do about it, though.
And sometimes her temp is a tad too high,
and sometimes she has a pain in her thigh.
It's a sharp pain (sometimes not).
It goes away only when
she applies something cold
and/or hot.

Oh! I also know the names of three of her doctors!
Shah, Gonzales, and Kenneth C. Koppernickel.
My gran has more doctors than a world-renowned hospital!

She's always got something that's out of sorts:

IBS, psoriasis, Mr. Plantar's Fine Warts.

But there's one thing I know that soothes every pain.

When I give her a hug,

Grandma feels right as rain.

Going

Summer camp starts tomorrow
and I'm GOING.
I don't know why, what, or who
or which-where-or-how . . .
There's so little about it I'm knowing.

It's supposed to be fun.
"Trust us, you'll see,"
but my concern is,
it possibly won't be.
And the only person I'll know
when I get there is *me*!

Do you think two weeks
is two weeks too long?
The only thing I'm sure of is—
I sure hope I'm wrong!

And Going

I'm sad now—who'd a thunk it?
Camp is over and I loved it.

The best thing about it,
other kids showed up, too!
And they also knew no one
and wanted to meet ME—someone new.

It was mostly outside and there was mostly sun.
We played lots of games and had lots of fun.
And we laughed from our bunk beds
by the light of the moon . . .
I'm GOING home now
and it feels too soon.

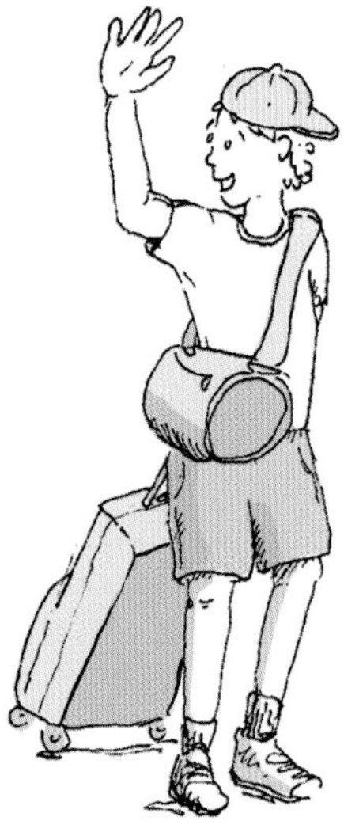

One More Thing!

"Get to bed," said my mother.
But I've got things to do,
a short list of things
that I'm getting right to.

Pick my socks up off the floor
Turn off all the lights
and shut every door
Make a cheese sandwich
Put on pajamas
Paint a quick painting
Write one more poem
Then gather my pals
for a show-and-tell show-'em

Learn a new yo-yo trick
and perform it, with feeling
Let the cat muffin my back
and count the cracks in the—

"ENOUGH!"
says Mom exasperatedly.
But, dear Mother,
you will love my last task,
though I do it belatedly—

One more chore
to finish my choring—
Jump into bed and get started on snoring!

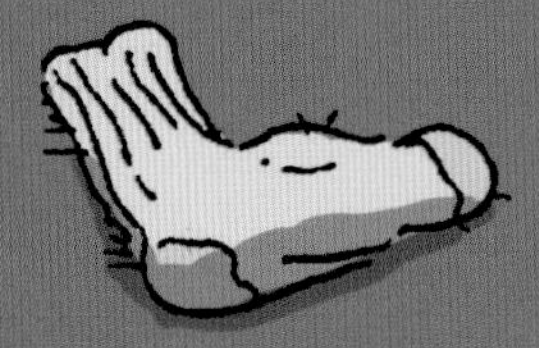

Umbrella Practice

Dad shouts, "Grab your umbrellas!
It's time for our practice!"
Mom says, "But we live in a desert!
Our yard's full of cactus!"

So for one minute only,
Dad sprays the hose like a geyser.
He gets soaking wet,
while we stay (somewhat) drier.

We practice stomping around,
making splishes and sploshes.
Someday we might live where it rains.
We might even own galoshes.

Dad warns us,

"Be prepared! You're not waterproof!"

He says it's his duty.

Mom says he's a goof.

I Flubbed It

I flubbed it.
I bumbled it.
I blew and I knew it.
I botched it.
I scotched it.
I whiffed,
muffed,
and fluffed it.

I flopped, majestically.
I came up short, most certainly.
I fell flat on my face.
The shame!
The disgrace!

Alas and dagnabbit!
Indeed and so be it . . .
I can't wait for tomorrow,
when I fully intend
to buckle in,
shake the dust off,
knuckle down,
scrape the rust off,
set to it,
get to it,
and do it again!

A Fly's Purpose

Why, oh why
do we need to have flies?
I simply must know.

That's easy—

because shoo-ing them

is a heckuva show!

mom

Dog Poop

You have a dog to be a friend.
To pet, to love, to take for walks.
You feed the dog and out comes poop
in slimy pellets or fulsome logs.

Don't touch it, please!
It's full of bacteria
and bacteria's bad.
It's full of disease.

Dog poop should be avoided—
Evaded! Condemned!
Let the adults pick it up.
That's why you have THEM.

TV Island

S.O.S.!
I did it again—
I'm all alone out here
without any friends.
It's just me and the remote
in my clicky little hand.

I started surfing about.
It was exciting, no doubt,
then I crash-landed.
Now I'm bored and I'm stranded.

I can't stop clicking.
Please don't scoff.
I need to stop clicking
if I hope to get off.

Take the clicker

or unplug the TV,

for I'm trapped,

lost, and lonely.

Oh, please come save me!!

The Pepper Man

Up to our table,
a suited sir stepped.
He offered us pepper,
the "freshest ever pepped!"

I waved my hand—no thanks, I'm fine.
But at that gesture, he began to grind.
He twisted his grinder . . .
So I waved some more
and soon, behold!
There was pepper galore.

He was determined.
I was entranced.
We both were captivated
by our little dance.
The pepper flakes floated down
like fluffy black snow
on the chickenny nuggets nestled below.
Soon, Pepper Peak was up to my chest
and the once-dapper pepper man
had sweat through his vest.

Finally, he ran out of pepper.
My wrist was strained
and a truce was called
on our flavorful game.
As our duet came to a finish
we were equally pleased.
We shook hands like gentlemen,
then both of us sneezed.

Pet Glacier

I adopted a glacier the other day.
I put a leash on it
so it can't float away.
Glaciers are melting.
It's upsetting and strange.
Our Earth is warming.
It's called climate change.
So I ate all the Popsicles,
tossed the mac 'n' cheese and the quiche,
and made space in the freezer
for my glacier on a leash.

It's a big job to turn the whole thing around.
I can't fix the whole planet
or even fix my whole town.

But I sleep a little easier

knowing it's true

there's a glacier in my freezer.

I hope you can help, too.

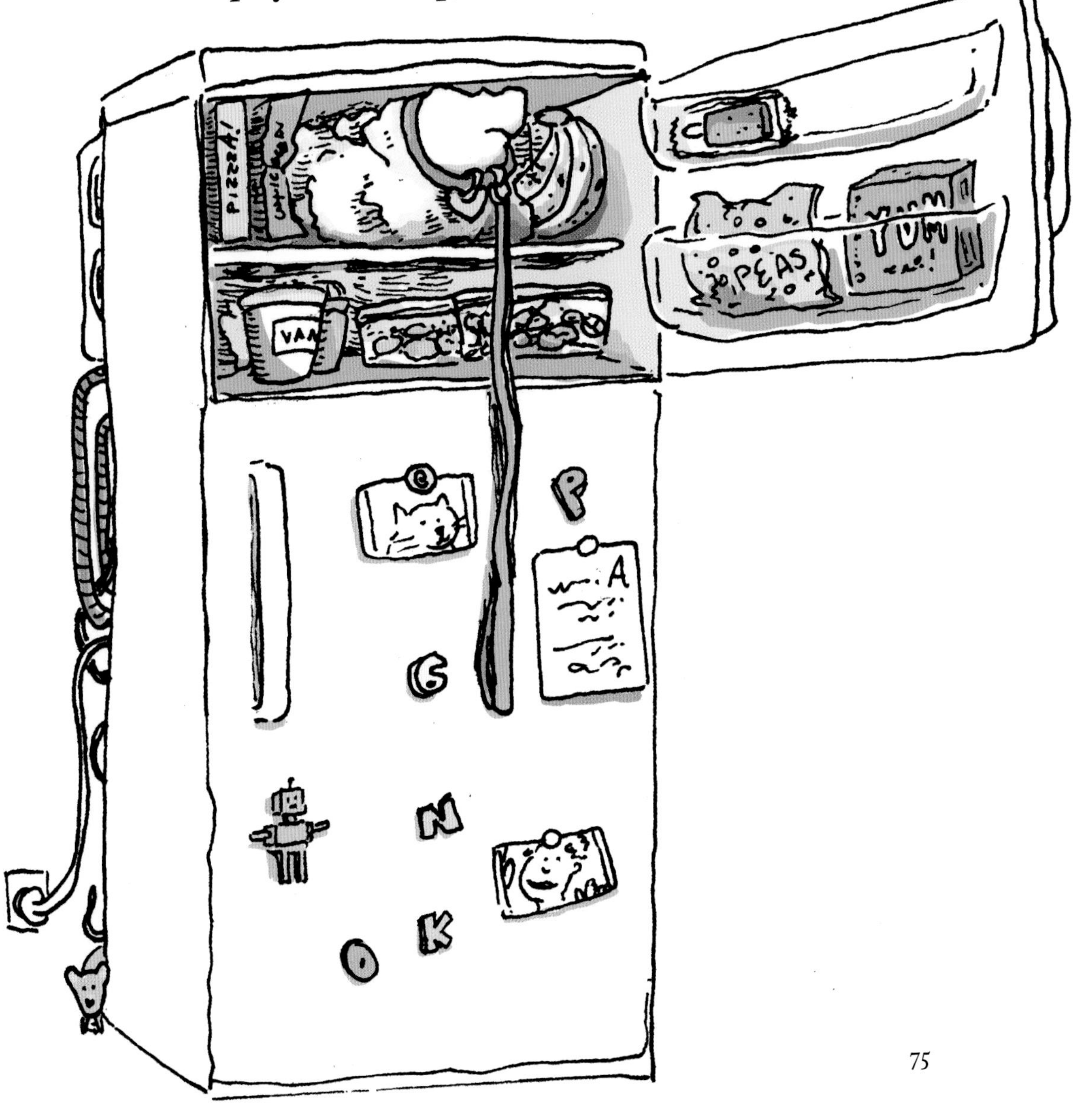

The Great Day

I was an awful good kid today,
or a "good awful" kid
might be a better way to say
that I was "terribly wonderful,"
"horribly great."
I started the day off by making us late!

I ruined the wedding, let's get it right out there.

I dressed fast,

nothing matched,

I combed not one single hair.

As always,

my big brother and sister looked perfectly right.

But this poem's about me and my sorry sight.

I ate a danish

as we drove to the church.

The car weaved and jiggled

and caused me to lurch.

The creamy cheese center

of the danish popped out

and landed on my trousers

and my shoes farther south.

(To be fair—some of the pastry made it into my mouth.)

I was sent to the bathroom to wash myself neatly.

I splished and splashed; I do nothing discreetly!

The bride joined me in the bathroom.

She was happy . . . I think.

In her high heels she slipped—

on my cream-cheesy ice rink.

Soaking wet, the poor lady, she started to bawl.

Her dress was a mess.

But wait, that's not all!

I was the ring bearer.

I dropped the rings down a grate.

As far as things going wrong,

I'd say that takes the whole cake.

Speaking of cake—

I bumped it a little . . .

The top tier collapsed

and married up with the middle.

Where there once were three layers
now there's just two.
But hey, the flavor's still great.
I checked it for you.

I give myself a gold star
for being me, today.
Who else could have done all that?
NO ONE, I daresay!

Tony Two-Feet

Tony Two-Feet
has got two feet,
ten toes,
thirty-two teeth,
and one nose.
A pair of legs,
a set of lungs,
a coupla hairs,
and a pinkish tongue.

This would be fine
were he like me,
for I am human, you see.
But Tony's a pigeon,
and for a pigeon,
he's more than a smidgen
un-pigeon-y!

Inside

Inside every child
who is jumping around
is a grandpa or grandma
desperate to sit down.

Trust me, though, when I say
that inside of old folks
moving careful all day
are vibrant, rowdy young-uns
hollering, “HEY THERE! LET’S PLAY!”

If you happen to find a sticky gum wad

- Raspberry Blue
- Expertly chewed
- Stuck under a table so I could eat food

IT'S MINE!

THERE'S A REWARD!

That's the big news...

Return it to me safely

and I'll share it wit' youse!

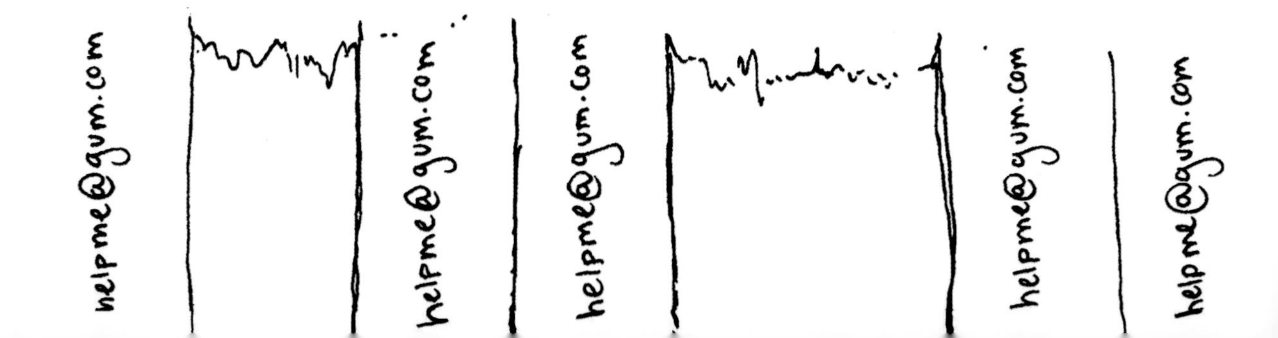

Shoe Tycoon

I see you are selling lemonade,
twenty-five cents a cup, and it's truly homemade.
Well, I'm setting up shop right nearby—
certified triple-A funky—
I hope you'll give it a try!

It's just ten measly cents.
Don't hold your pennies
so dearly.
I'm being sincere here.
I don't speak cavalierly.
Take a whiff of my insoles,
and you will breathe clearly.

The Tip of a Ship

In the sandbox
at the playlot
I dug deep down
and hit a jackpot.

A weathered bit of wood,
barnacle-crusty.
A treasure from yore,
sandblasted and rusty.

Yes, I knew without question
what I had in my hand.
Right here, in New Mexico,
so very far in-land—
the tippy toppy tip-toppety tip
of a mythically massive pirate ship!

And here it sits below me now,
the ship, its cargo, its aft and bow,
all the pirates' private things,
gold coins, gold buckles, and
golden rings,
a rudder, ropes, bailing buckets,
and pictures of their moms in
precious lockets,
and the cap'n's teacup, where he
was about to sip it
when the alarm bell rang and he
had to skip it.
Below me, all this booty lay
buried and forgotten to this very day!

"Ahoy!" I shouted.
What luck indeed . . .
Now I've got me own pirate ship
next time I be in need!
"Aaarrrrr . . ."

You Did It!

You did it! Look at you!
Above it all, what a view—
it's grander and beautifuler
than anyone knew!

You're so high up it's hard to breathe.
The air is thin; you gasp and wheeze.
But what's that smell? You can tell—
it's a wheel of cheese!
I left it for you—right over there.
Is it cheddar?
Is it Swiss?
No, it's called camembert!

Thank goodness the top of a mountain
stays awfully cold.
The cheese is still edible,
unmolded by mold.
You are equipped for this
with your crackers and knife.
Sit down,
have a snack,
then get on with your life!

I Like to Itemize

Let me itemize
by size
from my room all that I see,
categorize to emphasize
things starting with the letter *B*
(largest to small—listing them all).

Bed, Bookshelf, Beanbag chair,
Backpack, Boom box, Balloon, Bear,
Boots, Bunny, Bongo drum,
Biscuits, Brushes, Biscuit crumbs

When it comes to lists,
I'm prolific.
I'm deliberate.
I'm specific!

Some don't
understand,
they think it's
weird or funny.

But I'm the one
they come to
to
find
my
sister's
Bunny.

My Car

My car runs on turkey baloney,
carrot and broccoli stew.
When I drive it to Arizoney,
I can hear the engine chew.

BELCH

It's a Wand!

"It's a stick!" says Gary. "It's nothing!
Just a stick that's lumpy and rough."
I know it's a wand
and I know knowing's enough.
But Gary is the real dud.
He's a "stick,"
a "stick in the mud!"

Drippy Gary won't play along.
He's small-minded, it's tragic.
I know how to fix his wagon.
I'll summon up some magic.

I hex you now, Goofy Gary!

For I'm a real spell-spinner.

Not just tonight,

but for the rest of your life!

You shall be late for dinner!

For you see, when I pretend that a stick is a wand

I commit, I'm a "knower."

For the remainder of Boring Gary's life

he will eat only leftovers.

None for Me

"Dessert?" Mother asked me, with hope in her eyes.
I wanted to please her. So, I gave it a try . . .

My mother had baked a lemon muffin,
"tart" and "refined."
I tasted the top off it
and politely declined.

A cupcake came next,
a cream-filled confection.
I licked all the frosting
before it suffered rejection.
I sampled a snickerdoodle
and two chocolate pinwheels.
But when it came to cookies,
"No dice," and "no deal."

Mom's last great attempt,
her hope and her glory,
was an ice cream sundae
of no less than five stories—
three flavors, hot fudge,
and sprinkles galore.
I only ate most of it
and not a bit more.

Perhaps tomorrow I'll be in the mood.

We'll have to wait and see.

But, dessert, tonight?

"No thanks," and "none for me."

CH
VAN
AW
RRY
REAM
YUM

Later

LATER is coming.
Make no mistake.
NOW will not help you
to guess just how great
it can be
so much better
than YESTER, what's past
Don't look back, let's look forward.
Later comes slow, and then
FAST!

Sometimes you may wonder,
"Where's this Later?—It's late!
I want Later *Right Now*.
I've no time left to wait!"
But that ant in your pants,
I implore you, ignore it.
Later's coming, I promise.
Just stick around for it!

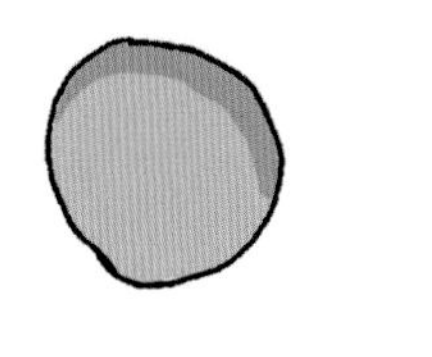

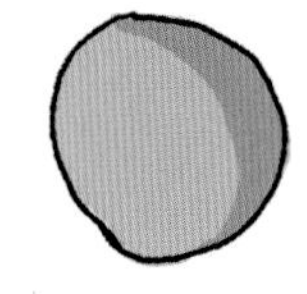
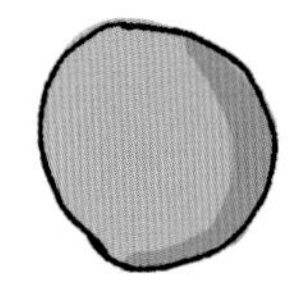
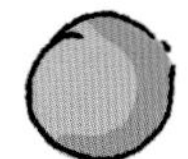

Science!

Clouds are made of cotton.

Dogs are made of fur.

Rocks are made of rock-hard something—

of that I am quite sure.

Boogers are made of snot.

Fish can breathe the water.

The sun emits yellow beams.

Older brothers are, generally, taller.

I'm a scientist, you see—

the world is my laboratory.

And I can tell you one thing true:

Skunks are made of stinky stuff.

I squoze one once,

pee-yew!

A Trip to the 99-Cent Store

A little of this and a little of that:

Some soap

A bandage

A cardboard hat

A roll of candy

A birthday card for "Mandy"

Marshmallow bunnies, marshmallow worms

Marshmallow marshmallows, marshmallow ferns

Three candles that sit in glass jars

Perfume-y trees to dangle in cars

A "No Trespassing" sign to hang on my fence

I can buy almost anything when everything's 99 cents!

Invisible Friend

My invisible friend is scared again
down here in Grammy's basement . . .
It's cold.
It's dark.
It's musty.
But he sticks with me 'cause he trusts me.

The thing is, he's afraid of ghosts,
which I do not believe in.
He's also allergic to dust bunnies.
(He sneezes when he sees 'em.)

He jumps when my shoes squeak.
He thinks my soles are haunted.
He suggests that we head back upstairs
but I remain undaunted.

The wind outside is howling.
The howl isn't helping.
I imagine he's imagining
a yeti baby—
yelping!

He's afraid of every little thing.
He gets pale and then goes whiter.
So why do we go to scary places?
We like when our hugs grow tighter.

Upside Right

A hat for my foot
set on top of my shoe
to keep the rain off it
and, when the sun's out,
keep it cool.

It's ridiculous,
some have said.
But not as ridiculous
as the shoe on my head.

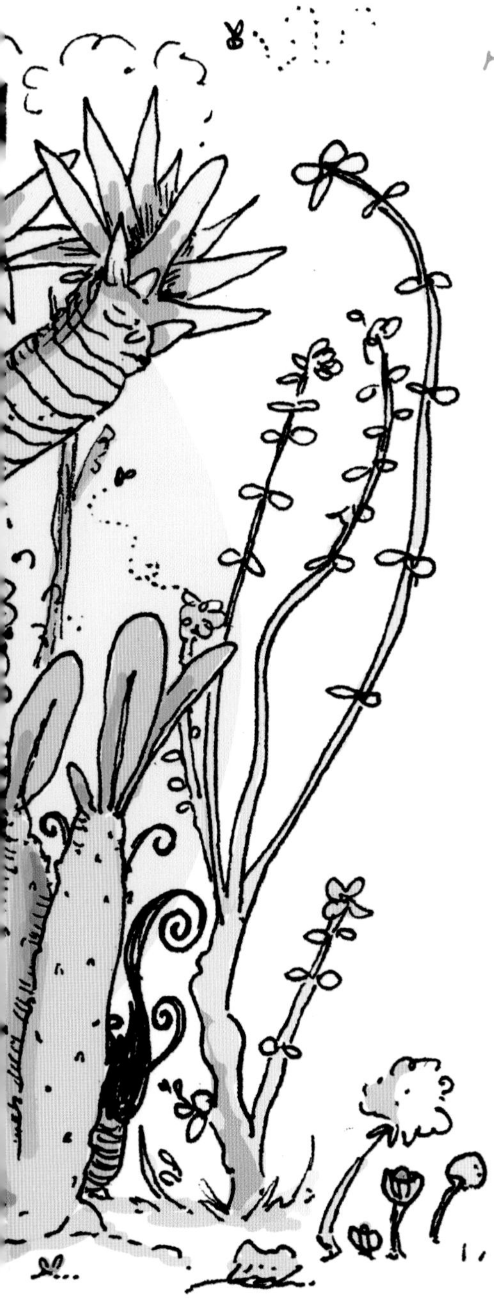

That Time of Year

A Red Barkling Elderblossom,
an Oak-Peppered Needling,
Pitted Swaying Swillows,
a Bumbershoop Seedling!

Look at the bushes, the flowers abloom.
Baby-Eared Bimpleberries,
a Flip-Capped Mushroom.

It's here, my dear, that time of year
when some folks do nothing but sneeze.
As for me, it's the season
when I have a reason
to invent all new names for the trees!

Grampa's Fine

My Grampa has an eggshell head
and a scratchy beard
and his breath is bad
and his elbow's weird.
Curly hairs spring from his nose,
but his eyes are sweet
(at least when they're closed).

He wakes up early
already smelling like coffee,
with notes of stinky sock
and just a hint of toffee.

A determined scowl alights on his face,
Gramps is off to lead the *slow-driving race*—

In the car he becomes a seether.
"No one knows how to drive!
Ride bikes! Or walk, either!"

We stop by the ice cream shop.
(That was never our goal.)
"I go where I want, when I want—
not when I'm told!
I want three scoops. I don't care that I'm cold!
It's no comedy show this 'gettin' old!'"
He still saves room for his dinner later today,
his onion-y favorite—creamy steak soissé.

When it comes to gripes and grumbles,
he's the number one champ,
the tippity-top grump,
and the world's best gramp.

Party of One

The table is set,

the chandelier is hung,

for my fancy, extravagant

party of one.

Chairs are put out.
The food's baked, broasted, and broiled.
The silverware's polished.
The lazy Susan's well-oiled.

No one's coming over.
No hurt feelings, I'm delighted.
I'll be rev'ling alone.
No one else was invited.

So why the big hubbub?
Am I getting married? No way.
And we're three-hundred-and-sixty-some days
from my yearly birthday.

In truth, I live simply.
I eat no more than I'm able.
I just love sitting down
at really long tables.

There, There, Little Monster

You snarl and grumble
and clack your teeth
and grunt and rumble
in the dark, beneath
my bed in the night.
As I'm falling asleep,
you chew holes in my socks.
Are they savory or sweet?

I've seen you hiding by the coat rack.
I've seen the bristly hairs on your back.
I see you, little monster!
I'm a fan of your lurk—
of your peeking! And sneaking!
All your monsterful work.

I glimpsed you most recently,
shaking and shivering.
Your eyes had a sad tinge.
Did I hear you whimpering . . .?
As I've come to know you,
you've grown scarcer, and wary.
I know what you're afraid of . . .
You're afraid you're not scary.

There, there, little monster.
No need to despair.
You keep being "scary"
and I'll keep acting scared!

Librarian Nancie

I hear a whisper from down the hall.
"Ahoy, readers!" is the call.
Our librarian Nancie is a sailor, after all.

She's got vim, she's got pep,
and a pretty bad sunburn on the back of her neck
'cause she spent all morning swabbing the poop deck!
But when she wants to read
her ship has a nook
perfectly sized for her and some books.
She adventures out to sea,
then adventures beyonder—
through tales below sails
her mind and soul wander.

Out at sea she eats healthfully,
avoiding scurvy and gout.
Upon her return she knows
all the best books for me to check out.

My Name

My name is long and lingering: Philleepeepoo Tippy-Tillering.
I prefer simply Philly,
and I don't mind Tip-Tillery.
When my second-oldest sister named me,
she was being quite silly.

Call me "Hey, you!" if that's for the best
or just "Peepoo!"
and leave out the rest.

Problem Solved!

"No problem was ever solved
by kicking and screaming,"
said my teacher,
the dignified Mr. Leaming.
But today I proved him wrong
with some tantrum-y scheming.

The problem I solved?
My favorite team was losing.
But then I got them to win
by stomping and whooping!

Dress for Success

A raincoat's a garment
for a rainy day.
A sunhat's the garb
to keep sunburn away.
Pajamas are suits
for going to sleep.
A wetsuit's the clobber
for exploring the deep.
But wearing a swimsuit
in a snowstorm that's freezin'
is not the frock, garb, or getup
you want to be seen in.

You'll be labeled
"a fashionable fool."
A contradiction—
for you'll be
both cold and uncool.

Zilot Return Policy

Unsatisfied with your purchase?
You can return this book fast.
Just follow our policy—
No questions asked!

The book must be sealed
in unpopped Bubble Wrap.
The whole thing vacuum-packed.
And PLEASE! *Not booby-trapped!*

The poems must be pristine and unread,
not one single rhyme
having entered your head.

If it's store-bought, return it safely
in its *original* bag,
and wear the same underwear
with *its* original tag.

Your refund will be issued
in the form of store credit
(NOT for the store where you bought the book,
one where you DIDN'T get it).

Include the receipt!
Signed by the store clerk,
and the pope, and the queen,
plus an original artwork.

Your return's nearly finished.
You're one step away,
and we sincerely apologize for any dismay.
One last thing you must do,
if you disliked it as much as you say:
Purchase two more copies
for your worst friends' birthdays!

Itch

I had a little itch
in the middle of my back.
I pulled a twig off an oak tree
and used it to attack.
I took heed of a sign
by the tree that said, *Touch me!*
What could possibly go wrong?
Not a thing I could see . . .

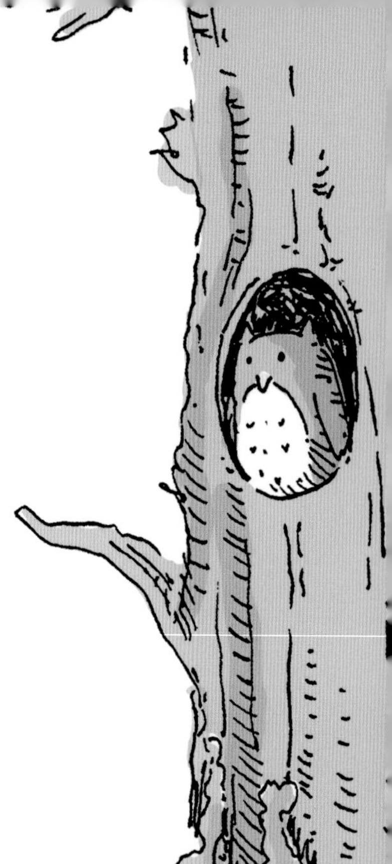

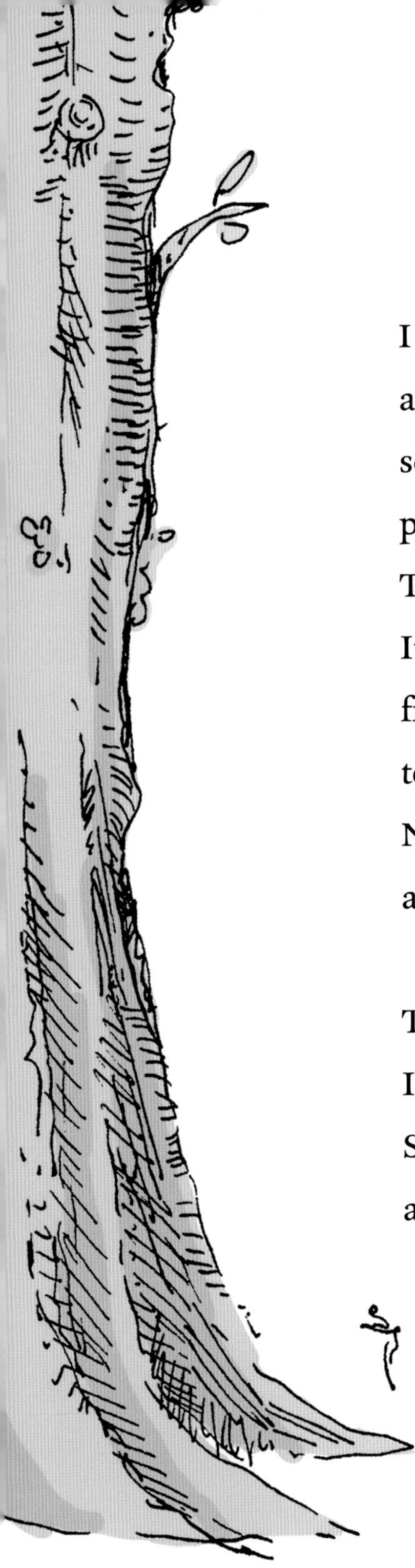

I scratched, then I scrutched
and skrappled away,
scritching my itch with great
pan-a-ché.
The more I scratched it, the wider it spread.
It spread and spread
from my back to my neck
to the back of my head.
Now I could put the twig down
and use my fingers instead!

The lesson I learned—
I'm happy to teach it:
Scratch your itch with the right twig
and you'll easily reach it.

A Little Night Music

Pardon me, but . . . is it so wrong if I sleep all day long
so throughout the night I can work on my songs?

I've been told that my singing
leaves people's ears ringing.
I bellow without restraint,
but my voice is not boring—
and it sure beats my snoring—
though it makes certain plants wilt and faint.

For the symphony sections
I'll cause ear infections
by crudely violining and fluting.
It might sound to you—to whom "music" is new—
like a whole lotta rooting and tooting.

And one final note,
to give you fair warning . . .
my trumpeting begins
at three in the morning!

A Sight to See

A piece of tape over a crack in the wall
tempted my curious left eyeball.
I unstuck the tape and what did I see?
A menagerie,
a panoply,
a hidden world—A SIGHT TO SEE!

A land of Oddfellows, I'll call them Squints
'cause I had to squint to see
their bony limbs and smiling faces,
when they noticed me!
Each Squint had arms—up to four or six.
Top hatted, bow-tied dandies.
Let me tell you, for this welcoming bunch,
multiple hands came in handy.

You see, the Squints I saw, they never stopped
doling out felicitations . . .
waving and calling “Hoi!” and “Helloi!”
among other unique salutations.
I was hailed as a friend!
As they wandered by,
they kissed and patted
my peering eye.
Floating by me in blimps
led by birds on long leashes,
I was lucky for the glimpse
of their outer reaches.

I would never have seen their world
if I hadn’t dared take a look.
But it’s a secret
so please keep it
’cause you’re the only one
who’s ever read
this poem on *this* page in *this* book.

Listen to Dr. Bluestone!

I've examined this child
and I won't sugarcoat it.
Take out pen and paper—
it's best if you note it.
The youth is sickly and weak,
something you must have suspected.
There's no fudge in their system!
At least none I detected.
This kid needs pizza,
and make it a staple.
For breakfast I prescribe pancakes
with syrup, strictly maple.

Popcorn at night!
With butter and salt—be generous!
At dinner, I implore you,
avoid all asparagus.
Have you administered any sprinkles lately?
They should be ingested daily.
Best on a sundae, or every day, just try it,
topped off with a cherry
to balance this diet.

I'm serious, I am! Why do you doubt me?
I may look young, but
don't make this about me.
My degrees are all real.
I'm not a concocter.
Now get the child a lollipop,
and one more for the doctor!

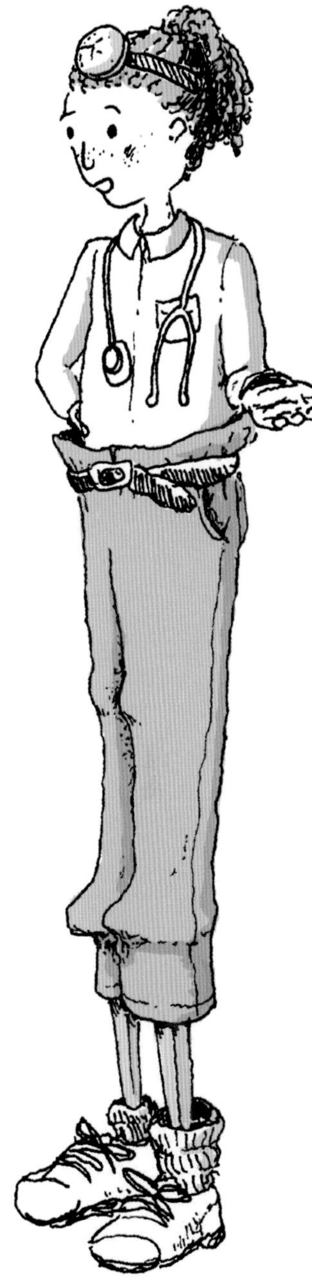

Order of Out

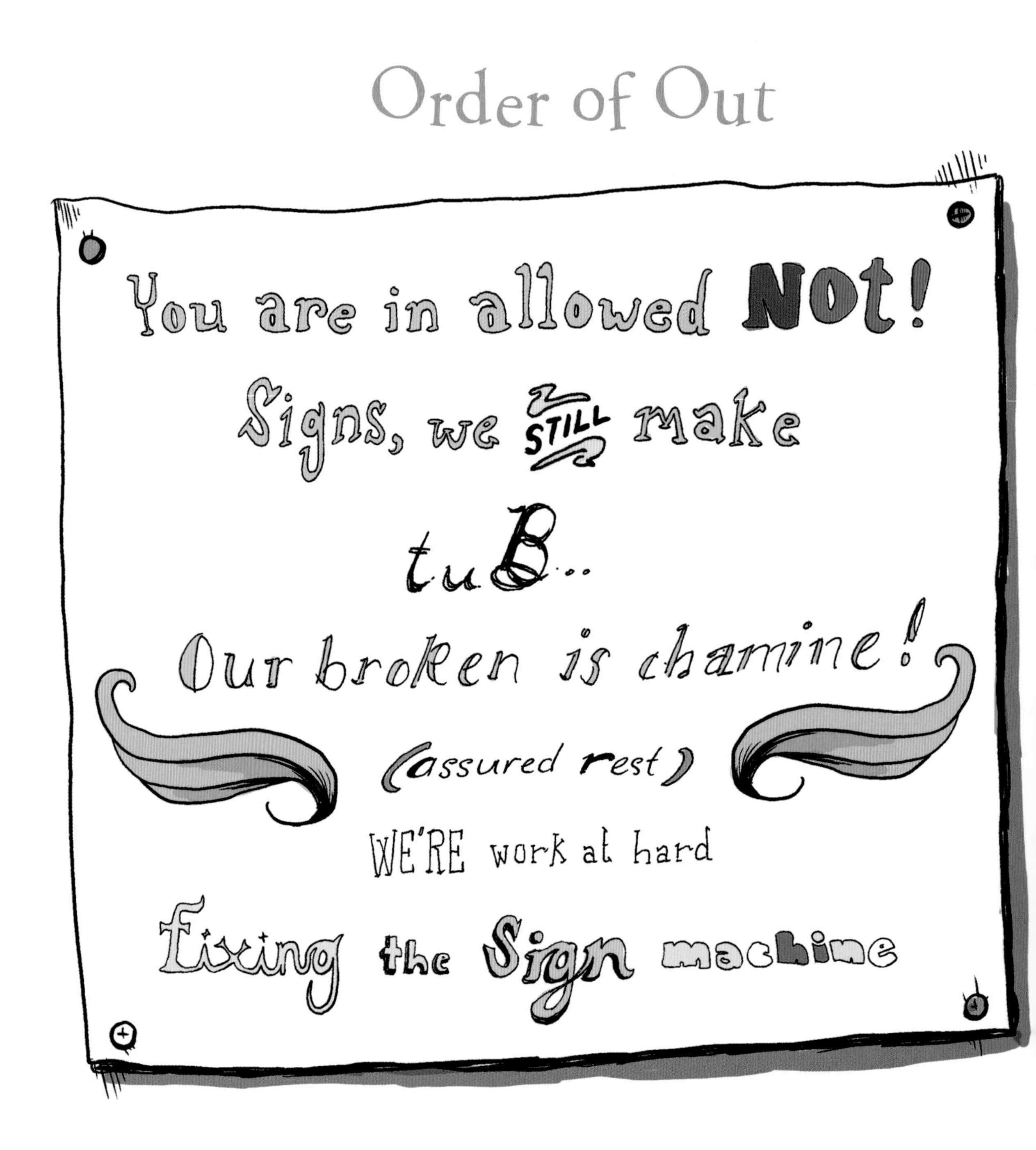
You are in allowed NOT!
Signs, we STILL make
tuB...
Our broken is chamine!
(assured rest)
WE'RE work at hard
Fixing the Sign machine

Leave Me Be

Don't feed me meat
while I'm eating my fig.
Don't step on my feet
while I'm dancing a jig.
Don't put gum in my ears
when I'm listening to music.
Don't pick my nose.
It's my booger. I'll choose it!

Guy in a Wagon

I'm a guy in a wagon
who's just sittin' still.
I'm feeling . . . what's the word?
Oh, yeah, "unfulfilled."

It's got working wheels
and a blanket for my butt.
I've got a snack in a bag,
a red grape and one nut.
And a bottle of water
so I can keep hydrating.
As I sit here expectantly.
Waiting . . . waiting . . . waiting.

I tell my dog Olive to "pull me, c'mon!"
One day she'll learn, she will.
But for now she just climbs on,
circles round and plops down.
Now there's two in a wagon
that's just sitting still.

Pledge

You!
Take this pledge with me
so friends we may always be . . .

I [me/you] pledge hereby
to be good and kind,
not sneaky or sly.
To play fair and not cheat.
And ne'er to lie.
And to put on clothes
before I go outside.
And if I must fart a whopper someday,
I shall wipe your tears
completely away.

I shall skip beside you,
pick you up if you fall,
and answer the phone with "Gobble-gobble"
whene'er you call.
And tip my cap to you,
and jump in the lake with you.
And if I bake a Bundt cake,
make enough Bundt for two.

I heretofore swear
to you and me both
to stand by and to honor
this grandiloquent oath.

A Cat Named Larry

A cat named Larry
had a mouse he carried
around with him as a pet.
His dad said, "Chase it!
Don't carry it.
You'll waste it!"
But he loved that mouse so very . . .
very much.

Well, cats live longer
than mice do, it seems.
Now Larry only sees his friend
in his kitty-cat dreams,
where they chase each other round,
never catching, that's okay.
It's the good feelings that remain
at the end of the day.

Poe Out a Poem

Write down what happened today
in a poem,
for all days are special
if you just get to know 'em.

ZILOT

Inventing Words

Did you read the ENTIRE book? Very cool . . .

Do you read books with your parents before bed?

Or on a rainy day?

Or even a sunny day when you need a break from all that sunny running around?

You *do* like to read a book or two?

Wonderful.

When my kids were little, we read a lot together. By the way, my name is Bob and I'm the dad in this story . . . and my wife, Naomi, the mom in this story, also read to Erin and Nate every day, even a few times a day. We liked reading in our house. Especially before bed.

We first looked at picture books, but then wordier books

came along. We read all the fun books, and very many silly ones, because those made us laugh, and, yes, there was often a lesson or a point being made, in even the silliest ones. But the laughter is the part I remember.

After we had read many books, I wanted to show my kids that somebody writes all these books. Some person. That person is called an "author," and while they may be a grown-up now, they were a kid like YOU once upon a time. All they did was write a few of their sillier thoughts down and then made a book of their own.

It's all made up . . . just like life.

Did you know you can even make up words?! My son invented the word *zilot* (/'zi-lit/) to name an "indoor fort," as described in the first poem in this book. Of course, you could just call it an "indoor fort" or a "blanket fort," but *zilot* is better and faster, and it made us all smile. So the word *zilot* stuck.

So there you have it . . . we created a word together!

We wrote these poems together.

You can do it, too.

We can't wait to read what you will write someday.

ERIN
ODENKIRK

Patty the Cat, Nate, and Erin before bedtime

Old Time Rhymes by Dad, Nate, and Erin

Old Time Rhymes

I made them up just now

a long long time ago

~~I know that~~

They're new to you

as you already know

They're true + honest

and make no sense

Fun for the whole family

except NO PARENTS

Acknowledgments

Thank you, Farrin Jacobs and Mary-Kate Gaudet at Little, Brown Books for Young Readers, for truly caring about each poem and each word in this book! You have been the most wonderful and giving partners in bringing the best out of us, and we will forever be in your debt. This book represents our team effort.

Thanks also to Erin Malone and Janine Kamouh, who helped us find a home at LBYR, and to Megan Tingley and Jackie Engel, who understood our collective vision and empowered us to build this *Zilot*. To Neil Swaab, who designed this book, and Sasha Illingworth, who art directed with the invaluable help of Patrick Hulse. To Andy Ball, Mara Brashem, Crystal Castro, Marisa Finkelstein, Amanda Gaglione, Alice Gelber, Virginia Lawther, Kayleigh McCann, Martina Rethman, and everyone else involved in getting this book into the hands of readers! Thank you, Emilie Polster and Cheryl Lew, for spreading the word out to the world. And special thanks to Victoria Stapleton for working with teachers and librarians to encourage kids to write their own poems.

And thanks, too, to our favorite authors and illustrators—the people whose books inspired us to write our own: Calef Brown (*Dutch Sneakers and Flea Keepers*), Mark Alan Stamaty (*Who Needs Donuts?*), Dr. Seuss (nearly all), Shel Silverstein (*The Giving Tree*), Jane Yolen and Kathryn Brown (*Eeny, Meeny, Miney Mole*), Tony Millionaire (*Sock Monkey*), Susan Meddaugh (*Beast*), Chinlun Lee (*The Very Kind Rich Lady and Her One Hundred Dogs*), and so, so many more.

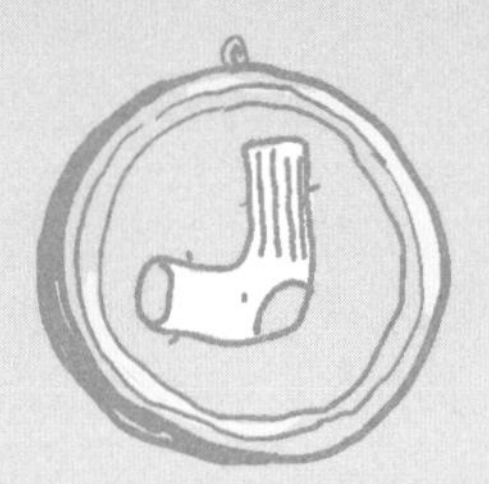

STRAW

MOM

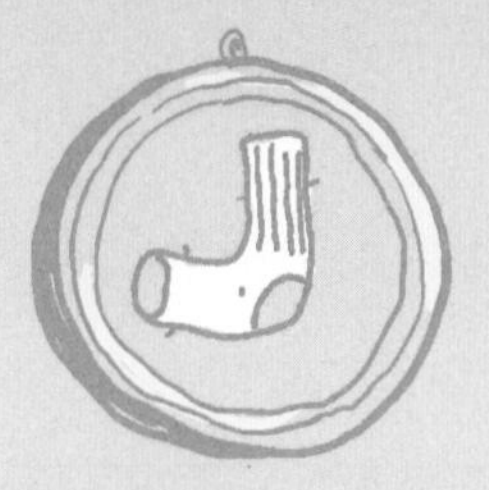

STRAW
BERRY

MOM

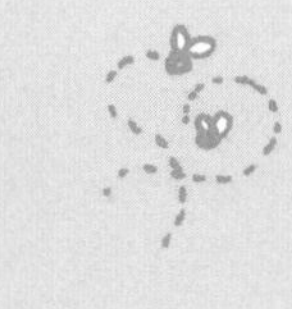

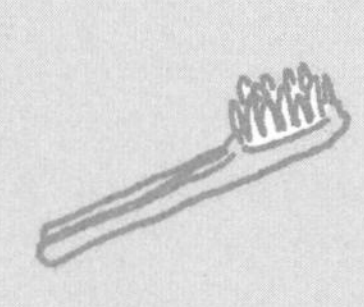

LOVE